Henry Wadsworth Longfellow

HIAWATHA

Pictures by SUSAN JEFFERS

SCHOLASTIC INC.
NEW YORK TORONTO LONDON AUCKLAND SYDNEY

For my friend Sheldn

ISBN 0-590-46238-5

 Published by Scholastic Inc., 730 Broadway, New York, NY 10003, by arrangement with Dial Books for Young Readers, a division of Penguin Books USA Inc.

12 11 10 9 8 7 6 2 3 4 5 6 7/9

Printed in the U.S.A. 08

First Scholastic printing, September 1992

Sincerest thanks to Helen Burnham and the staff of the Croton Public Library.

Henry Wadsworth Longfellow's interest in Native American culture began many years before his epic poem, *The Song of Hiawatha*, was first published on November 10, 1855. Longfellow had known the chief of the Ojibwa tribe and had seen the last few Algonquins in Maine. He had read the work of Henry Rowe Schoolcraft, an American ethnologist who had lived with the Ojibwas, and had spent many hours composing sketches and contemplating the best way to approach a subject he felt deeply about. On June 22, 1854, the following entry appeared in Longfellow's diary:

I have at length hit upon a plan for a poem on the American Indians, which seems to me the right one and the only. It is to weave together their beautiful traditions into a whole. . . .

The figure of Hiawatha himself was to be a composite character constructed from the stories Schoolcraft and others had set down. One such story concerned an actual man named Hiawatha, a chief of the Onondaga tribe who was known for his diplomacy in forming the Iroquois nation.

The poem that finally emerged was unlike anything previously published. After combining the various myths, legends, and first-person accounts written by others, Longfellow added his unique sensibility and made the material his own.

Longfellow was well-loved and respected during his lifetime, and when *The Song of Hiawatha* was published, he already enjoyed a considerable reputation. So it isn't surprising that the poem was an immediate popular success both in America and in Europe. One of its admirers was Oliver Wendell Holmes, who described it as "full of melodious cadences."

I was first introduced to *The Song of Hiawatha* as a child. It had always been a favourite of my mother's, and she loved to read me the section about the young Hiawatha that began, "By the shores of Gitche Gumee. . . ." Soon the lovely imagery began to enter my daydreams; I even remember sneaking off into the woods behind our house, where I'd pretend to be a woodland Indian who talked to birds and listened to the wind blow.

I came upon the poem again two years ago, and as soon as I reread it, I knew I wanted to illustrate the section that I'd loved as a girl. Before starting my sketches I tried to become as familiar with my subject as possible. I made numerous trips to the Museum of the American Indian in New York City and took rolls of photographs of artifacts, clothing—anything that seemed interesting, unusual, or beautiful. I pored over Schoolcraft's writings, Edward Curtis's photographs of Native Americans, George Catlin's wonderful portraits, as well as his first-person accounts, and Longfellow's other poetry. But more important I read and reread *The Song of Hiawatha.*

Although I chose to concentrate on the section about Hiawatha's boyhood, I hated to sacrifice the poem's epic quality. It occurred to me I could distill the essence of the preceeding verses on the first double page spread and in the illustration for the dedication page, and provide a sense of what was to come in the last illustration. Thus, the first picture shows Nokomis, the "daughter of the moon," falling to earth after a jealous rival has cut her heavenly "swing of grapevines." It is followed by a painting of the daughter she bore, Wenonah, as she lies dying of a broken heart because the mighty West-Wind has deserted her. Wenonah's son is Hiawatha, and her spirit watches over the boy in the next few paintings. The last illustration pictures Hiawatha as a young man; Nokomis's friend Iagoo is giving him his first bow and arrow.

As I sat thinking about the art for the book, I felt a strong link to the wonder I'd had as a child. In these paintings I've tried to recapture some of that feeling and add it to the rich landscapes and noble people that fill Longfellow's great poem.

Susan Jeffers

By the shores of Gitche Gumee,
By the shining Big-Sea-Water,
Stood the wigwam of Nokomis,
Daughter of the Moon, Nokomis.

Dark behind it rose the forest,
Rose the black and gloomy pine-trees,
Rose the firs with cones upon them;
Bright before it beat the water,
Beat the clear and sunny water,
Beat the shining Big-Sea-Water.
There the wrinkled old Nokomis
Nursed the little Hiawatha,
Rocked him in his linden cradle,
Bedded soft in moss and rushes,
Safely bound with reindeer sinews;
Stilled his fretful wail by saying,
"Hush! the Naked Bear will hear thee!"
Lulled him into slumber, singing,
"Ewa-yea! my little owlet!
Who is this, that lights the wigwam?
With his great eyes lights the wigwam?
Ewa-yea! my little owlet!"

Many things Nokomis taught him
Of the stars that shine in heaven;
Showed him Ishkoodah, the comet,
Ishkoodah, with fiery tresses;
Showed the Death-Dance of the spirits,
Warriors with their plumes and war-clubs,
Flaring far away to northward
In the frosty nights of Winter;
Showed the broad white road in heaven,
Pathway of the ghosts, the shadows,
Running straight across the heavens,
Crowded with the ghosts, the shadows.

At the door on summer evenings
Sat the little Hiawatha;
Heard the whispering of the pine-trees,
Heard the lapping of the waters,
Sounds of music, words of wonder;
"Minne-wawa!" said the pine-trees,
"Mudway-aushka!" said the water.

Saw the fire-fly, Wah-wah-taysee,
Flitting through the dusk of evening,
With the twinkle of its candle
Lighting up the brakes and bushes,
and he sang the song of children,
Sang the song Nokomis taught him:
"Wah-wah-taysee, little fire-fly,
Little, flitting, white-fire insect,
Little, dancing, white-fire creature,
Light me with your little candle,
Ere upon my bed I lay me,
Ere in sleep I close my eyelids!"

Saw the moon rise from the water,
Rippling, rounding from the water,
Saw the flecks and shadows on it,
Whispered, "What is that, Nokomis?"
And the good Nokomis answered:
"Once a warrior, very angry,
Seized his grandmother, and threw her
Up into the sky at midnight;
Right against the moon he threw her;
'T is her body that you see there."

Saw the rainbow in the heaven,
In the eastern sky, the rainbow,
Whispered, "What is that, Nokomis?"
And the good Nokomis answered:
" 'T is the heaven of flowers you see there;
All the wild-flowers of the forest,
All the lilies of the prairie,
When on earth they fade and perish,
Blossom in that heaven above us."

When he heard the owls at midnight,
Hooting, laughing in the forest,
"What is that?" he cried in terror,
"What is that?" he said, "Nokomis?"
And the good Nokomis answered:
"That is but the owl and owlet,
Talking in their native language,
Talking, scolding at each other."

Then the little Hiawatha
Learned of every bird its language,
Learned their names and all their secrets,
How they built their nests in Summer,
Where they hid themselves in Winter,
Talked with them whene'er he met them,
Called them "Hiawatha's Chickens."

Of all beasts he learned the language,
Learned their names and all their secrets,
How the beavers built their lodges,
Where the squirrels hid their acorns,
How the reindeer ran so swiftly,
Why the rabbit was so timid,

Talked with them whene'er he met them,
Called them "Hiawatha's Brothers."

Ye who love a nation's legends,
Love the ballads of a people,
That the voices from afar off
Call to us to pause and listen,
Speak in tones so plain and childlike,
Scarcely can the ear distinguish
Whether they are sung or spoken;—
Listen to this Indian Legend,
To this Song of Hiawatha!